RENARD
THE
FOX

by Rachel Anderson and David Bradby

illustrated by Bob Dewar

Oxford

Oxford University Press, Walton Street, Oxford OX2 6DP

Oxford New York Toronto
Delhi Bombay Calcutta Madras Karachi
Kuala Lumpur Singapore Hong Kong Tokyo
Nairobi Dar es Salaam Cape Town
Melbourne Auckland

and associated companies in
Beirut Berlin Ibadan Mexico City Nicosia

OXFORD is a trade mark of Oxford University Press

Text © Rachel Anderson & David Bradby 1986

Illustrations © Bob Dewar 1986

First published 1986

ISBN 0 19 274129 2

British Library Cataloguing in Publication Data

Anderson, Rachel
Renard the fox. — (Oxford myths and legends)
I. Title   II. Skir le renard. *English*
823′.914[J]   PZ7
ISBN 0–19–274129–2

To Claudine and Joël Masson
who lent the table

Typeset by Oxford Publishing Services

Printed in Hong Kong

Adam, Eve, and Renard

At the beginning of the world, Adam and Eve were turned out of the garden of paradise because they cheated against God's rules. But they looked so helpless that God took pity on them and gave them a special stick.

'Any time you need anything,' he explained to Adam, 'You just strike the sea with this stick and you'll get whatever it is you want.'

So Adam and Eve went down to the beach. Adam grasped the stick in his hands and struck the water with it while Eve stood and watched.

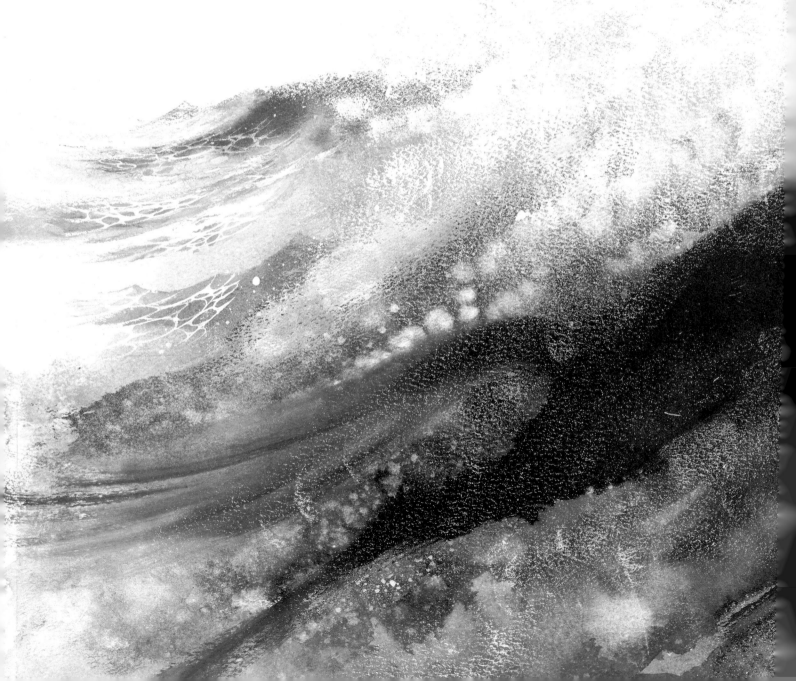

Immediately a sheep came trotting out through the waves.

Adam said, 'Now my dear, this is a sheep. You take it, and you look after it for us, and it'll give us milk and cheese, and it'll also be good company for you.'

Eve thought to herself that if one sheep could provide milk, cheese and companionship, two sheep would be even better, so she grabbed hold of the stick for her turn at hitting the water.

But this time, a wolf came bounding out from the sea. The wolf saw the sheep, rushed at it, seized it by the throat and began to run off towards the forest with it. Eve was surprised to see their first animal

being carried off by the second and she started to shriek and yell for help.

Crossly, Adam took back the stick and once more struck the sea.

At once a dog appeared. The dog saw the wolf in the distance and immediately gave chase. When the wolf heard the dog in pursuit, then felt it snapping at its hind legs, it loosened its grip on the sheep's throat. But as it ran off alone through the trees, the wolf thought to itself that, if given half a chance, it would certainly try again to get that sheep.

Meanwhile the dog, having rescued the sheep, led it back to Adam and then ran round Adam's legs wagging its tail with pleasure at its own achievement.

So Adam now had a sensible dog as well as a docile and companionable sheep. He was almost happy and didn't feel half so bad about being turned out of the garden of paradise. He and Eve decided to call more creatures out of the sea. Each time that Adam struck the water a quiet useful creature appeared through the waves. And each time that Eve struck the water a savage beast rushed out and ran away into the forest like the wolf.

Adam's creatures, the cock, the cat, the pig and the hen, were quickly tamed and grew to like living near humans. Eve's beasts were all rogues.

Among Eve's wild rogues was a four-legged creature, not unlike the wolf. But instead of having black hair, this one had reddish hair and it was extremely clever. It was more cunning than any of the others, either Adam's or Eve's. And its name was Renard the Fox. So that's how it all began.

Wolf and Renard the Fox were at first friends. They had both been summonsed from the sea by Eve and so, once in the world, they ran wild together. Together, they rested. When they were hungry, together they stole and killed and shared whatever they had. But it couldn't last like this always. Neither liked having to share, and so after several generations, the friendship between wolves and foxes began to sour.

Renard and Wolf

ONE day, Renard the fox saw the priest hurrying across a stubble-field towards the village. The priest was on his way to take a choir practice. Renard noticed that he carried a heavy wicker basket which looked as though it might contain food. The priest lifted his skirts to climb over a stile into the next field and Renard observed that as he jumped down the other side, something fell out of the basket, but the priest, not realizing, hurried on.

Renard was hungry. He was often hungry. Spring, summer, autumn and winter, he was on the look-out for something to eat. He ran round the edge of the field to the style, slid under it, and found what the priest had dropped. It was a bundle of something wrapped in a clean cloth. Inside the cloth, Renard found a lot of newly-baked fairy cakes, at least a hundred of them. Since he was so hungry, he immediately ate

all but two. He put these last two into the side of his mouth to keep in case he got peckish again later on.

Soon he met his friend the wolf.

'Hello there, old chap!' he said (with some difficulty because of the two cakes pouched in his cheeks).

Wolf was in no mood for cheery how-do-you-do's. He had been hunting day and night, had not found a single thing to eat, and was ravenous and miserable.

'Then you must certainly share my fairy cakes,' said Renard, dropping them out of his mouth.

'Ooh, cakes!' said Wolf. 'Where on earth d'you find those?'

'Just on the ground. Hidden behind a corn-stook for me to find. Look, since you're my best pal, you'd better eat them both. Even if they were the last morsels left in the world, I'd want to give them to you.'

'That's very civil of you, Renard. You're a true friend. But at least let's go halves, One each.'

'Not at all, You're obviously the hungriest. I insist you have both.' Renard said nothing about having already eaten ninety-eight cakes.

'Any more?' said Wolf when he'd gobbled down both fairy cakes. 'They were very good, but not very filling and I'm still famished.'

'No,' said Renard. 'Those were the only two I found. But I think I know where they came from.'

Since it was the priest who had dropped the cakes, Renard thought that there might well be more of the same inside the church. 'You follow me, Wolf, and I'll see what we can do.'

So Renard led Wolf down to the church on the edge of the village, but the door was locked.

'Never mind,' said Renard, and he found a small hole under the church steps. 'Get digging, Wolf, and we'll tunnel our way in.'

Inside, the church was empty and silent. The choir had long since finished their practice and gone home. So had the priest. However, heaped on the chancel steps, were not only a quantity of little fairy cakes, but big cakes too, and also huge loaves of bread, and baskets of fruit, cheeses, a side of ham, sheaves of wheat, some punnets of blackberries, several pumpkins, pots of greengage conserve, and three flagons of cider.

'Oh, I say! Renard, my friend!' said Wolf who was very impressed. And Renard too was astonished to come upon quite such a splendid spread set out, more than enough for the two of them.

'What a good chap this priest is to keep such a well-stocked church,' said Wolf. 'And look, he's left us some wine too, hidden in this chest.'

Wolf couldn't wait to begin. 'Pull up a pew, Renard. Make yourself at home,' he said, sitting down in the middle of the display and tearing off a piece of bread, gobbling some cheese and gulping down some swigs of wine.

But Renard, who was not as hungry as Wolf, was disgusted to see his fellow scavenger slurping and burping in such a greedy way.

'Hold on, Wolf. Not so fast. Remember, this *is* a church. You ought at least to try to eat nicely,' he said and took a clean altar cloth from the chest, unfolded it, and spread it neatly on the floor. But Wolf was too busy eating and drinking to bother with dainty manners. He stretched over for more cheese, fell on a pumpkin, and knocked over a basket of plums. Wine dribbled down the hairs of his beard. Crumbs were caught in his ears.

'Renard, my best of companions, drink up now. It's not like you to be timid where food and drink's concerned. Don't be shy now. Look, I'm ten drinks ahead of you already!'

'Steady on. Don't get too carried away.' Renard felt uneasy about eating all the church food.

'But why else do they keep this food in here if it's not for us to enjoy?' Wolf said as he started on a side of ham.

'It's for the priest to use when he's saying Mass of course,' said Renard.

'Then we too shall say Mass,' said Wolf. He was becoming so drunk that he could hardly see straight. His eyes were popping out of his head like live red coals. 'You won't believe this, Renard, but I used to be a choirboy when I was younger. I can probably remember a tune or two from the past. We'll have a bit of a sing-song, bring back some of the old ones, eh?'

'Wolf!' said Renard sternly. 'You can't sing hymns looking like that, you old scruffbag. It'd be an insult to a church to stand up there singing when you look such a mess.'

'Tidy me up then, my good friend! Give me a short back and sides!' In the vestry, Wolf found a pair of scissors and a comb which were used to neaten up the choirboys before a service.

Wolf was becoming unsteady on his legs. He had to put out a paw against the vestry wall to stop himself falling over. As he did so, he noticed a row of hooks and hanging from the hooks, the choirboys' robes. Wolf struggled himself into a red cassock and pulled on a white surplice over the top. He found a starched white ruffle for his neck.

'Tie it for me, Renard,' he said.

'That's all very well, Wolf,' said Renard. 'Wearing the clothes. But you can't start a service now. The bells haven't even been rung.'

Renard had no wish to be caught in a church with a drunken wolf.

'Oh, let me do it! Let me ring them at once! Ding dong bell, pussy's in the well! Oh, this is fun, Renard! Aren't you enjoying it!' Wolf staggered to the bell tower at the back of the church and seized hold of the bell ropes. First he tolled a funeral knell, then he rang a peal, then he did both together. 'Oh glorious noise! Let steeple bells be swungen. Now let all good people come to church and hear me preach.' Wolf

tottered up the steps of the pulpit, threw back his head, and began to howl. It sounded like a whole pack of wolves in considerable pain.

Meanwhile the priest in the presbytery next door heard the clanging of the bells and called the curate and the housekeeper.

'I think there's thieves in the church,' he whispered. 'We must take care.'

So each grabbed a weapon — a stick, a broom, a candle-snuffer. The priest unlocked the church door and peered in uncertainly. As soon as he caught sight of Wolf in the pulpit with his coal bright eyes, his disarrayed robes, and harvest produce scattered all down the aisle, he knew it was the devil.

'There he is!' he cried. 'Bringing corruption and outrage into our holy church.'

The people of the village, roused by the bell-ringing, crowded in behind the priest armed with rakes and hoes and spades. The noise of

their chattering stopped Wolf's singing. Seeing them armed to the teeth and surging towards him suddenly sobered him up.

Renard didn't like the look of the crowd either and felt it was high time he made his get-away. He dodged between the people's legs and away through the tunnel under the church steps.

'Hey! wait for me!' stammered Wolf and tried to wriggle after Renard. But he was hampered by the voluminous choirboy robes and by the ruffle getting in his eyes. 'Wait, Renard,' he wailed. 'Help me. Give me a hand.'

'Tough luck, old pal. Can't wait. As you sow, so you must reap.'

The crowd was warming for a good fight and when they saw how all their harvest decorations had been ruined, they rushed at Wolf shouting and screaming with fury. They beat Wolf about the head and back and would probably have tried to kill him, but just in time he made a flying leap for a high-up window-sill, heaped with red apples. He pushed open the window and jumped for safety. Then, still wearing the

13

choirboy cassock and surplice, he ran as fast as he could for the woods.

'It's all that Renard's fault,' he muttered to himself. 'He lured me into that church in the first place. I bet he did it on purpose, just to get me into trouble. He might at least have waited to get me out of the pickle. The trickster. If I ever see him again, I'll get even with him.'

And at that very moment he saw Renard quietly resting under an oak tree.

'Ah, there you are, dearest Wolf. Welcome back to safety. I'm glad you're all right.'

'I'm not on speaking terms with you!' screamed Wolf furiously. 'You evil red-haired dwarf! You ran out on me! You left me alone! I had to defend myself against hundreds of the enemy! *And* they beat me black and blue!'

Since Wolf had behaved so disrespectfully in the church, Renard thought it probably served him right. 'Wolf, dear friend,' he said. 'You've got it all wrong. I was waiting for you all the time, just outside the tunnel, all ready to pull you out, but you never came. You should have trusted your best pal. Still, you got away with the choirboy's robes, I see. They should fetch a decent price. And since I shared my fairy cakes with you, we'll split the profit on the sale, won't we? And you never know, we might even manage to sell them to the priest, make him buy back his own choir's clothes. That'd serve him right for getting you beaten up, wouldn't it? Come on, let's go to market rightaway.'

'Oh very well,' said Wolf irritably.

Renard and Crow

THE crow was hungry. He'd had nothing to eat for days, or so it seemed to him. He flew out from the wood and, to his amazement, in a clearing, he came upon a thousand freshly-made cheeses spread out on the ground.

They were rich, yellow, with a fine aroma, and they'd been put out in the autumn sun to dry.

Crow darted quickly down from the tree and snatched one up in his claws. Immediately, an old woman to whom these thousand fresh cheeses belonged rushed out from her cottage.

'You scum!' she shrieked, and threw stones into the air at him. 'You filthy sneaky thief! Bring that back this instant!'

'Old woman,' called Crow from the safety of a branch. 'If I were you I'd save my breath to cool my porridge. If you wish to start discussing cheeses with me, you may certainly do so. But you aren't getting this one back in a hurry. Right or wrong, for better or worse, it's mine now. Finders keepers, losers weepers. If you were so worried about your precious cheeses you shouldn't have left them lying about like that. You offered me a very good opportunity to help myself, which I wisely did. It was entirely your own risk to leave them on the ground like that. However, if you want my advice, I'd watch a good deal more carefully over the other nine hundred and ninety-nine. The one I've got here has an extremely good flavour. I dare say the rest have too. Well, I must be off now. It's been nice talking to you. So long!'

And he flew back into the deeper woods, settled onto an upper branch and began to devour the cheese in peace and comfort.

As Crow, at the top of the tree, satisfied his hunger, he was quite unaware that, at the bottom of the same tree, lay Renard the Fox. Renard was half-asleep. He was feeling exhausted and slightly bruised from an incident in a market place with an angry priest. Because of this incident, and the need to escape quickly, he had had no time to look for food. He hadn't had a bite to eat for days, or so it seemed to him. So when a small crumb of rich, yellow cheese fell through the air and landed on the ground right by his nose, his life immediately began to improve. He sat up and looked round to see where this heavenly gift had come from. And, on looking up, he saw the crow on the branch with a fresh yellow cheese clutched in his claws.

'Why hello there, Mr Crow,' Renard called up politely. 'Can it really be my dear old pal Crow? For goodness' sake what a happy chance meeting you today. Gosh, how well I do remember your late-departed father, Mr Crow Senior, may God rest his soul, known in his time as one of the very best singers in all France.'

Crow didn't answer. He was busy with the cheese.

'You know, Crow, you too as a child, sang exceedingly well. I wonder if you still have the gift. It would be interesting to find out. Do sing me a small refrain if you have the time. It'd be so good to hear your sweet tones again.'

At first, Crow ignored this invitation to show off, but then he

couldn't resist a quick trill, and so left off eating for just long enough to croak a brief scale.

'Good Lord!' said Renard, 'That was fantastic! 'You know, Crow, you actually sing even better now than you used to, though I dare say if you really put your mind to it you could probably reach even higher notes.'

Crow, pleased with the noise he had just made, began to squawk loudly and happily.

'God Almighty!' cried Renard. 'It is astonishing. How clear and clean your voice is. And could be clearer still if you gave up eating walnuts which, I'm told, tend to stick in the throat and irritate the vocal chords of the world's top singers. Even so, despite your eating habits, I'd rate you among the ten best in the world. Do sing just one more time, for me.'

17

Such continuing flattery of his hideous voice was more than Crow could ignore and he began to bellow louder than ever and so lost his grip on the cheese and let it slip from his grasp. It tumbled through the branches to earth and landed exactly in front of Renard.

But Renard, although hungry, did not so much as sniff at it. He had further plans. A half-eaten fresh cheese was all very well. But what would be even better would be a half-eaten fresh cheese followed by a fresh plump bird.

So he eased himself away from the cheese as though moving caused him great pain.

'Oh Lordy, how little happiness I have in this world. And on top of that, this cheese really stinks to high heaven. I can hardly bear the pong. It's making me feel quite ill, as though I didn't have enough to put up with already. I'm already under doctor's orders, you know. He's absolutely forbidden me to touch cheese until I'm quite recovered from my injuries. So I wonder, dear old Crow, if you'd please be good enough to hop down here and defend me from this appalling over-ripe dairy product. Obviously, I wouldn't normally ask such a thing of you,

but you see one of my legs seems to be broken. I'm virtually immobile. I shall doubtless have to remain in exactly this position until the doctor has set me in plaster. Even then, I'll have to stay without moving till I'm quite restored.'

Renard liked the part he was playing. Somehow, he even managed to make a few tears of self-pity trickle from his eyes. And Crow, seeing Renard weeping and moaning and ignoring the cheese, began to be taken in. Branch by branch, he hopped further down the tree, though he didn't come too close because he knew that Renard often had a few spare tricks at the ready. Crow stopped just beyond Renard's reach.

'Dear friend,' Renard coaxed, 'Don't be afraid. What harm can a poor broken-down fox do you?'

But then, instead of waiting until Crow was within his certain reach, Renard made a false move. Too soon he leaped up and snapped at the bird so that instead of catching the whole bird in his jaws, he only managed to grab a mouthful of feathers.

Crow flew back up to the highest branch croaking angrily, furious both with Renard and with himself.

'Oh God, what a fool I was to be taken in by all that smooth talk. And look what you've done! You've maimed me! Four feathers gone, two off my tail, and two off my right wing, so I'll be all lop-sided till they grow again. You can have that damned cheese for all I care. But you're certainly not persuading me to get near you again. Once bitten twice shy, I'd say. I was mad to believe in that false limp of yours.'

At first Renard didn't bother to reply because he was too busy wolfing down the cheese. It was fresh, rich and good. In fact, the only thing wrong with it, in Renard's opinion, was that there wasn't quite enough.

'I'd say, Crow,' he said as he licked round his muzzle, 'that I've never eaten such an excellent cheese since the day I was born. And it's done me the power of good, quite restored me to good health. I'm feeling as fit as a fiddle. So I'll be on my way now, dear Crow. Until we meet again.'

'Not if I can help it,' croaked the Crow.

Renard and Heron

RENARD lay under a bush, exhausted. The hunting season had begun. For three days the Royal Hunt had been on his tail in full cry, with horses, hounds, knights and men. And he'd been so busy giving them the slip, that he'd had no time to worry about rest or food for himself or his family.

But at last, the hounds called it a day and went off into the forest after some poor old stag, which gave Renard time to catch his breath.

From beneath his bush, he suddenly noticed that a heron was standing on one leg in the river nearby.

'Well, well, well,' thought Renard. 'Only drawback is, Heron's downstream over on the far side, and I'm upstream and here. And I'm not even sure if I know how to swim.'

Renard watched Heron staring intently into the flowing water. Heron suddenly dipped his pointed beak, his neck, and his head deep into the water to pierce at a fish.

'Though I suppose,' thought Renard, 'that if I were to lie quite still and wait and wait, there's a million-to-one chance that Heron might choose to wander over in this direction and do his fishing on my side of the river. Though I have no doubt that while I was waiting and waiting

for my moment to pounce, some meddling peasant would come along and interfere in some way.'

Heron went on fishing for his supper and Renard went on watching with longing, and as he watched, he tried to work out how he could trap him for his supper.

Finally, he had a plan worked out. He crawled through the undergrowth to the edge of the river bank. There he pulled off a handful of bracken stalks which he wove together into a small raft shape and pushed it out into the water. He watched it float gently away from him and downstream towards Heron.

Heron, totally absorbed in his fishing, was startled when a raft floated up. But when he realized that it was only a heap of broken bracken drifting by on the current he went back to his fishing.

Renard made a second raft of bracken, larger and stronger than the one before, and threw that into the water. This time, Heron took more notice. He paused in his fishing, strode through the shallows to it, picked it over with his beak, searched through it with his claws and only

when he'd seen that there was nothing to be alarmed about, nor anything worth eating, did he once more resume his contemplative fishing.

Renard made his third and final raft, this one the largest of all, more like a nest than a raft, and woven from bundles of autumn-coloured bracken which exactly matched the colour of his own brown fur. In the centre of this nest-raft was a fox-sized hollow of exactly his own size.

Renard hesitated for a moment before stepping into the nest-raft because he wasn't entirely sure if it was strong enough to bear his weight, nor had he convinced himself of his own ability to swim in the event of accident.

However, he plucked up his courage. 'Nothing venture, nothing gain, and never say die,' he said to himself as he cast off.

This third raft was carried, like the previous two, on the current down to where Heron still fished. But Heron, already interrupted twice by heaps of floating bracken, this time took no notice whatsoever.

'Hm, hm, I've better things to do with my time than peck around at useless bits of floating debris,' he said to himself. 'I mind my own affairs,' and he once more plunged his head under the water to spear a fish. Immediately, Renard leaped out from the nest-raft and, seizing Heron by the neck, dragged the bird up the bank and behind the nearest bush. Heron squarked with rage and indignation as best he could considering there were long sharp teeth at his throat. But Renard, having himself been hunted prey for three long days, was not in a tender mood. Holding his victim firmly with his front paws, he finished him

off with a quick bite in the gizzard.

Evening was falling and a harvest moon was rising as Renard finished his supper. But he decided it might be safer to sleep off this enormously satisfying meal before going home because he knew how dangerous it can be to start a long journey on a full stomach, or at any rate that's what he'd heard people say. So he curled up in a heap of straw and slept soundly till dawn, when he awoke from a frightful nightmare in which he dreamed his home was on fire.

He said a quick prayer. 'From all the terrors of the night, and of the early morning, please keep me safe, O Lord. Amen.'

On opening his eyes, he was astonished to find that, far from being scorched by flames, he was surrounded by water. The straw stack, in which he had gone to sleep the evening before, was no longer in a field beside a peaceful river but was floating right in the middle of a swollen and flooded river. He was drifting helplessly, miles from home and out of reach of either bank.

'Why on earth didn't I go straight home to my darling wifiekins last

night, then I wouldn't be adrift here in the middle of nowhere.' Remembering that he probably couldn't swim either, Renard prepared to give up the ghost and go the way of all flesh.

At that very moment a small boat came by and the man rowing this boat spotted Renard crouched in the straw.

'What a lucky stroke this is!' said the man. 'Good old Saint Julian!' (Saint Julian happened to be the man's favourite saint.) 'A fox! A very good fox indeed, with a perfect pelt. Just the thing. I could sell the brown fur for a fair whack, and keep the pretty breast fur to trim my jacket for winter. And then I'll chuck the carcass back in the river because I wouldn't want fox meat stinking the place out.'

At the thought of being skinned alive, and then having his hairless body thrown in the water, Renard's resignation to death by drowning disappeared and his resolve for survival returned.

'Not so fast, my man,' he thought. 'He who laughs last laughs longest.' And Renard had every intention of lasting and laughing longer than anyone.

The man in the boat changed direction and began to row rapidly towards the floating strawstack. He then reached out both his hands to grab Renard by the neck. Renard dodged. The man lifted one oar to stun Renard by bashing him on the head. But Renard did an agile half twist and avoided the blow and the oar fell overboard. The man turned, lunged again towards the fox. Again, he missed.

'Third time lucky,' he muttered with an evil glint in his eye. 'This time I'll have you.' He pulled off his wooden clogs, scrambled to the bows of his boat, and made a great leap right into Renard's floating strawstack. But the instant that Renard saw the man coming at him, he took a flying leap over the man's head and landed in the rowing boat. He seized hold of the remaining oar and pushed off.

'One two three, and you can't catch me!' he yelled at the astonished boatman as he poled himself vigorously to the far bank. And on reaching the security of dry land, Renard bounded all the way home as fast as his legs would carry him.

Renard and Wolf go Fishing

THE people in the village were busy stocking their store-rooms with bacons and hams all ready for the Christmas feasting. But Renard had more interesting things to do with his time than fretting about food for some future date. With the coming of the cold weather he'd thought up a great new winter trick to play on Wolf.

He invited Wolf to go fishing with him. Once bitten was not, in Wolf's case, twice shy, Wolf had a very short memory. He took Renard at his word and completely forgot about the incident in the church.

They arranged to meet near the village pond at dusk.

It was a clear starry night with a hard frost. The pond was frozen solid, apart from a single hole which the village people had cut in the ice in order to be able to draw water for their livestock, or rather those of their livestock which weren't to be salted down for the store-rooms.

Wolf went to the pond, as agreed, and saw Renard already waiting for him out on the ice.

'Hello, Uncle Wolf!' called Renard.

'I'm *not* your uncle,' said Wolf.

'Well never mind, come on over here anyway, and just take a look at this splendid fishing hole I've found.'

Wolf crossed the ice carefully to where Renard stood by the hole. The villagers had left a bucket in the water hole too.

'Couldn't be a more perfect spot for night-fishing, could it?' said Renard.

'But what do we have to do?' Wolf wondered. 'How do we get at the fish?'

'Well, look, the kind people have left their thingy, their, er, what-have-you for us.'

'It's a bucket,' said Wolf. 'In the water.'

'Ah yes, but it's a very special bucket. A particular fishing tackle kind of bucket for winter use. And this hole is just brimming over with eels and sprats and kippers and cockles and mackerel and tunafish. You'll get a beautiful bucketful before you can say Jack Robinson.'

Wolf was dopey and hungry. 'Thanks, Renard, for telling me about this great place. Quick, you fix the fishing bucket onto my tail.'

'Your tail?' said Renard. 'Very well.' Since Wolf had actually asked him to, he attached the Wolf's tail firmly to the handle of the bucket.

'Then let it down into the water for me,' said Wolf.

Renard did so.

'What happens next to get the fishing thingy full?' Wolf wondered.

'Well, as far as I know,' said Renard, 'you have to sit on the ice and wait very very quietly for the fish to come swimming along and into the bucket.'

So Wolf obediently sat on the ice with his tail dangling into the cold water and the bucket on the end while Renard went and lay under a bush, rested his muzzle comfortably on his front paws, and waited and watched for the next stage in his trick on Wolf.

As the night grew colder, the water in the drinking hole began to freeze over and, as it froze, the bucket and Wolf's tail which was attached to the bucket became fixed firmly in a trap of solid ice.

Wolf began to think he'd had enough of fishing.

'Hey, Renard!' he called. 'I reckon I've had enough of this fishing lark!'

'All right,' called Renard. 'I expect you've caught quite enough by now. We'd better be off before first light or those infernal huntsmen will find us.'

But when Wolf tried to get up he found that he couldn't move.

'Renard, brother, friend! Help me. Wait for me. I'm stuck. I think

27

the bucket's too full.' However much he twisted and turned, he couldn't free himself. His tail was gripped firmly in the ice as though by powerful teeth.

'Bad luck, chum,' Renard called. 'But it's no good crying over spilt milk. Worse things happen at sea. Anyway, that's what comes of being greedy. He who wants most, usually ends up with nothing!'

Meanwhile as the winter sun rose over the white and frozen horizon, the lord of the manor ordered the horses and called up the hounds. It was a perfect day for hunting. Renard, hearing the distant cries of hounds, shouts of men, and calls of horns, retreated at once to the safety and comfort of his lair.

Wolf too could hear the sound of approaching danger but he was struck fast, as though rooted to the pond.

A kennel boy was first to spot him. 'It's the wolf! The wolf!' he cried and immediately the greyhounds were unleashed and came bounding over the snow, then onto the ice, slipping and sliding. They were fierce. Wolf was fiercer, lashing out with snaps and bites and snarls.

His lordship dismounted at the edge of the pond and came skidding over the ice. Wolf watched him draw his sword and braced himself for death. But as his lordship raised the weapon, he slipped and lost his balance. His lordship slashed out with the blade but didn't kill Wolf, only cut his tail through almost to the bone. The pain was terrible but the injury had at any rate one merit in that it released Wolf from the ice in the nick of time.

His lordship was hopping mad with himself for his carelessness in missing (though not half as angry as Wolf was with Renard). His lordship scrambled to his feet to strike again but Wolf wasn't quite so stupid as to stay around and wait to be slain at a second attempt. Leaving the better part of his tail behind, he ran away across the ice and into the forest.

'That wretched evil worm!' he snarled to himself. 'The skunk, the swine, the cheating scab! Next time he won't get away with it. One of these fine days I'll get my own back. Then he'll be sorry.' And he disappeared among the trees, still howling with pain and rage.

Renard Changes Colour

RENARD was not pleased. The King had declared him an outlaw, so he'd have to be more cautious than usual in his travels.

To protect himself from anything too dreadful happening, he went to a little hill, turned to the east and quickly prayed a small prayer which turned out to be surprisingly effective.

'Dear God in Heaven,' he prayed, 'you have already saved me from quite a pack of nasty things and you have also forgiven me for a whole load of my naughty tricks. Perhaps you'd be able to do me another favour and give me a little disguise so that nobody will be able to see who I am. Thanks in advance. Amen.' Renard bowed again to the east before setting off in search of a meal.

And, though he knew he was now wanted, dead or alive, he was so hungry and there was so little to eat in the countryside, that he risked a trip to town where the pickings were usually better. But it didn't seem to be his lucky day. Even in town, he found nothing to scavenge. Then he came to a house where a window had been conveniently left wide open. Since he could see nobody inside he jumped in through the window. Just underneath the window was a huge vat of yellow dye and Renard fell right into it. He sank immediately to the bottom. When at

last he bobbed back up to the top, he splashed and thrashed and gasped and choked as he tried to prevent himself from drowning because he realized that he couldn't swim.

The dyer who mixed the dye, and who had only gone away for a moment to fetch his measuring stick, was annoyed when he came back to find an exhausted animal churning around in his nice new vat of dye, and he naturally tried to bash the animal on the head with the measuring stick. But Renard called out:

'Dear sir, please don't do that, for though I'm not human but an animal, I'm in the same trade as you, and you surely wouldn't want to hit someone from your own profession? As a matter of fact, I know quite a few tricks of the trade which I could pass on. I bet you don't know about mixing your dye with wood ash, do you now?'

'No, I don't,' said the dyer. 'But what I really want to know is what on earth are you doing in my vat?'

'Ah, now. There's a good question. I was mixing your dye for you properly in the new approved method. It's the way they do it in Paris these days. Since I've now thoroughly stirred it for you in the Parisian style, perhaps you'd please help me out, and I'll tell you what else to do to be ahead of the fashion.'

Renard held out his paw and the dyer pulled him out.

As soon as Renard was on firm ground again he changed his story.

'Well, ta very much and all that, and now I suggest you'd do better to take care of your own business and don't go around trusting it to a fox. Because I don't know the first thing about the dyer's trade. Though I do know one thing. Jumping into your wretched vat has nearly finished me off. Practically drowned in the stuff. But I'll say this for you. Your dye seems to be pretty good quality.' The colouring had taken so well on Renard's fur that he was a bright canary yellow. Outside in daylight it seemed even brighter. The more Renard looked at it, the more pleased he was with it, so much so that he soon forgot about his hunger.

His good spirits couldn't last for long, however, because just outside the town, he caught a glimpse of Wolf lying under a hedge, and Wolf was big, strong, stupid, and fierce. Wolf had only half a tail too, owing to an incident on an icy pond.

'Oh, no!' thought Renard. 'Once he sees me I'm as good as dead.' But, to his surprise, when Wolf caught sight of him, he bowed politely and greeted him respectfully.

'Good day to you, sir,' he said to Renard and to himself he mumbled, 'What a fabulous-looking creature! So very yellow and so distinctive. Obviously a stranger in these parts.'

'That's all very well,' thought Renard. 'But the moment Wolf hears me speak he's bound to recognize my voice and be down on me like a ton of bricks.'

'I believe, sir,' said Wolf, 'from your appearance that you must be from another land? You are not French I imagine?'

'No. Me no good speakie you lingo.'

'Ah. Then where are you from, sir?'

they had to tip-toe quietly for, as Wolf explained, the owner of the guitar had a very fierce mastiff dog which slept by the fire.

'You wait here, Trotter,' Wolf hissed, 'and I'll get the guitar for you. He always keeps it hanging on a nail against the wall.'

'No, no, nein, nein, non! Please, Sir Wolf, no leavy me alone!' said Renard.

'What? You afraid of the dark, then?' said Wolf. 'Well, I'd always heard that musicians were drips, but I must say, I'd never believed it.'

'Not me scared *dark*. Me scared big bad outlaw. Maybe he come get me. That bad Rellart.'

Wolf laughed. 'It's not Rellart. It's Renard. But don't worry, if he comes, I'll soon take care of him. Now you sit quiet and I'll fetch that nice guitar for you.'

Wolf crept to the bedroom window of the house. It had been most conveniently propped open with a bit of stick. Wolf climbed up onto the sill and jumped in. He crept across the floor and unhooked the instrument from the wall. He crept back across the room and handed the instrument out through the window and down to Renard, who hung it by the cord around his shoulder so that he looked like a real singer-minstrel. Since Wolf was still inside the house, Renard had the brilliant idea of making the most of it.

'I can really make a fool of him!' he thought to himself. 'Too good a chance to let slip.'

He quickly knocked away the stick which held open the window, so that it slammed down and shut fast.

Wolf, inside, was terrified out of his wits to find himself suddenly trapped inside a darkened house. He gave a growl of fear which woke the owner of the guitar who started screaming and shouting at the top of his voice.

'Thieves! Robbers! Burglars! Murderers! Spies! Assassins! Wake up, wife! Wake up, children!' And even though Wolf slunk into the shadows, the mastiff smelled him and bounded over and bit him hard on the bum.

The man ran outside his house and yelled louder than ever, and soon the whole street was awake. A crowd rushed with sticks and clubs to help their neighbour chase Wolf out of the house.

Wolf saw the front door open and made a dash for it, only to run straight into the armed crowd in their nightshirts who chased him across the courtyard, down the street and out of town.

Meanwhile, Renard made the most of the house being empty to dart in and seize a ham which was hanging from a beam, ready for the family's Christmas feast. Then he danced all the way out of town to a

quiet spot where, having eaten the ham, he strummed himself a tune on the stolen guitar.

'Wassail, wassail, all over the town!
Our bowl is white and our ale it is brown!'

When the sun came up in the East, on Christmas morning, Renard bowed low and said his prayers.

'Dear Lord, thanks for answering my request so faithfully. Amen and a happy Christmas to you.'

Renard, Sheep, and Donkey

ONE morning Renard woke up with a brilliant idea. He decided to make a New Year's resolution. He decided that he wanted to live his life quite differently from now on.

'I've done so many terrible things,' he thought. 'I've stolen, and I've murdered, tricked and thieved. I don't suppose I've eaten a single meal that I haven't first pinched from somebody else. It's extraordinary to remember all those happy hens and delicious ducks, and cheery chickens, and bantams, and chicks, pecking away quite contentedly till I came along. Though at least I can say that I always gave them a good quick death so they didn't have long to suffer. But from now on things are going to be better.'

So he set out on New Year's Day to begin living his new improved life he planned. But as he trotted along, he began to remember more of the wicked things he'd done. And the more he thought about his past, and the hundred hens who could never now forgive him for what he did to them, the sadder he became.

A peasant passing by even noticed tears in Renard's eyes.

'Hey you, Fox!' he called. 'Why are you crying?'

'Because there's nobody left in the whole world who can still trust me. And I've decided that I must put all my old life behind me and start afresh.'

'Don't make me laugh, Fox!' said the peasant. 'What d'you take me for? Some kind of fool? I'll bet this is just another of your clever tricks. You'll never change your ways.'

'But it's true! Cross my heart and hope to die. I'm turning over a new leaf. I'm going straight to find a holy man who I can confess everything to.'

And to show he really meant it, he went immediately to a chapel in a clearing in a nearby wood.

'Oh, blimey!' said the priest. 'Not you again! What on earth are you doing back here? The last time you were in these parts, you nicked all my ducks. Be off with you, Fox!'

But Renard fell at the man's feet, pleading for mercy.

'Oh, very well then,' said the priest. 'Confess all your sins if you must. One at a time. But don't take all day about it.'

'Well you see, it was like this,' Renard began. 'I first began my life of crime when I was quite young. I used to pinch chickens wherever I found them, even if I wasn't feeling hungry. I crept up on them really cunningly. Another sin I remember is how I broke a promise to one of my friends and then bashed him on the head. I've also committed numerous daylight robberies and I've cheated old ladies, even stolen from women and children. Gosh, I've done so many awful things that I probably couldn't get through telling you in a month of Sundays.'

'With a record like yours, there's only one thing for it. You must go on a pilgrimage and confess to the Pope,' said the priest.

'All the way to Rome? But that's rather a long way for a fox.'

'Too bad,' said the priest. 'Either you're truly sorry or you aren't.'

'All right,' said Renard. 'If you say so.'

He found himself a pilgrim's cloak and set off. But very quickly he grew tired of travelling on his own, so he was extremely relieved when he came to a meadow full of sheep grazing.

A ram lay in the middle of the flock, so Renard stopped for a chat.

'Hello, Mister Ram,' said Renard. 'What are you doing lying there when everybody else in your field is eating?'

'Resting,' said Ram. 'I'm exhausted. From looking after all my wives.'

'But life is for living, not for lying around doing nothing!'

'You don't know the half of it,' said Ram mournfully. 'I'm owned by a terrible master who works me far too hard. Ever since I first learned to bleat he's been putting me in charge of huge flocks of sheep. D'you know, I'm father of every single lambkin you can see in this field? And d'you know what else? Just because I'm getting old, he's promised me as shepherd's pie to his workers, and he's offered my fleece to some gentleman or other who wants fancy fluffy sheepskin shoes to wear when he goes to Rome.'

'Rome! But that's just where *I'm* going.'

'Oh, I see. I wondered why you were all dressed up like a pilgrim.'

'Why don't you come along with me? Much better than waiting here till you're turned into fancy shoes. You come and enjoy a bit of fun while you're still alive. Even if they don't make you into shoes right away, they're bound to bump you off when it gets round to Easter time. They really go in for mutton then. You come along with me and nobody'll be able to turn you into boots.'

So Ram was persuaded. But the two pilgrims had hardly gone any way when they met a donkey in a ditch eating thistles.

'Hello,' said Renard.

'Hello,' said the donkey. 'Oh, it's you! What are you doing all dressed up like that? Playing pilgrims?'

'I'm not playing. I *am* a pilgrim. Haven't you heard? I've turned over a new leaf. You see, God actually *prefers* bad people like me to all the good ones. It says so somewhere in the Bible. Ram's a pilgrim too. We're going to Rome. I don't suppose you'd want to come too? No, you haven't the stamina. I dare say you prefer slaving away, year in, year out, for some wretched master.'

'I wouldn't mind coming with you,' said Donkey. 'Provided I knew that there'd be enough to eat.'

'Of course there will. More than enough. People always give charity to pilgrims.'

So the three pilgrims went on, and by nightfall they had got as far as

the edge of a huge dark forest. And, by the sound of things, it was a forest full of ferocious beasts.

'Pilgrim brothers,' said Ram, 'where are we going to sleep? It's getting late.'

Donkey agreed with Ram that it was high time they found somewhere safe for the night.

'Dear friends,' said Renard, 'what better hotel could there be for simple pilgrims like us than God's own sweet grass beneath God's own noble trees?'

'I want a proper shelter,' said Ram.

'Me too,' said Donkey.

'Because I bet this forest is full of wild animals,' added Ram.

'Yes,' said Donkey. 'So do I.'

'My friends,' said Renard, 'your wish is my command. Of course you shall have proper shelter. Very near here is the house of a friend of mine, Wolf.'

'Wolf?' said Ram who had a particular distrust of wolves because of something which had happened many generations before to one of his ancestors.

'Yes, he's a really good pal. Never lets me down, and he knows about the importance of giving hospitality to holy pilgrims. He's bound to put us up for the night.'

The three pilgrims went to Wolf's house but he and his wife were out. So Renard went in and began to look for food. There was salt meat, several kinds of cheese, and a wide variety of green stuff to suit all tastes. They also found plenty of beer.

Ram drank so much beer that he began to sing. He had a deep bass voice. Donkey drank so much that he began to bray. He had a tenor voice. And Renard drank so much that he sang falsetto. They could have gone on all night, happily singing in harmony, if Wolf and his wife hadn't decided to return from their evening's hunting. Wolf was carrying a carcass in his mouth.

Hearing the singing coming from his own house, Wolf said, 'People!'

His wife peeked through a hole in the wall and saw the singing trio grouped around the fire.

'But that's wonderful, dear,' she said to her husband. 'What a piece of luck! Ram and Donkey and that wretched Renard, all sitting there like that, just waiting for us to grab them.'

And so Wolf and his wife rushed at their front door to get in and seize their victims. But the door was locked from the inside.

'Open up!' shouted Wolf.

'You must be joking!' called Renard from the inside.

'Renard!' shouted Wolf. 'I order you to open up my front door. If you don't, I'll kill you. And your friends.'

'Oh, dear,' said Ram. 'We're really trapped now. There's no escape for us. Once they get in it'll be curtains for us.'

'Don't be silly,' said Renard. 'I can easily get us out of here in one piece, provided you listen carefully and do exactly what I tell you.'

'Yes,' said Donkey. 'We will.'

'Right. Now you, Donkey, are the strongest. I'll lift the latch for just long enough for Wolf to poke his head through. Then you bang the door shut again as hard as you can so his head is wedged in, but the rest of him is still outside. Got it?'

Donkey did as he was told and as soon as Wolf's head was caught in the door, Renard shouted at Ram to charge. And when Ram had charged once, Renard gave the order to charge a second time, and a third, again and again. Ram was like the country's finest battering ram attacking the defences of the strongest fortress.

Wolf saw stars and then fainted clean away. His wife went howling off into the dark forest and began to assemble a whole pack of relatives. In less than an hour she'd assembled a team of over a hundred.

When Renard, Ram, and Donkey left Wolf's house, the pack easily picked up their scent.

'Come on, you two. If you want to get away alive, you must put on a bit of speed,' he said.

But Donkey only brayed with fright. 'I can't go any faster than this. I've never been taught to gallop.'

Renard could see there was no way Donkey's short little legs would ever run fast enough to escape.

'Well in that case, there's only one thing for it,' said Renard. 'We'll have to climb this tree. Then the wolves will lose our scent.'

'But I can't climb a tree!' said Ram. 'Nobody ever taught me.'

'Nobody ever taught me either,' said Donkey.

'It's never too late to learn,' said Renard. 'As you can hear, Mrs Wolf is extremely angry with us, so I suggest you both start learning now. You'd be surprised what can be achieved in times of crisis. If faith moves mountains, it also helps rams up trees.'

Renard scrambled up the branches as high as he could go.

'Now you two, follow. Come on. Climb, climb. Up up up. Use a bit of will power.'

When they saw there was nothing for it, they followed him up, and clung to a branch out of harm's way.

By the time the wolves reached the tree, their three victims were out of sight, and the wolves couldn't understand why they had suddenly lost the scent of their quarry.

'They've probably gone underground,' said Mrs Wolf. 'We'll wait.'

The hundred wolves lay down and, being tired out by the fast chase, they fell asleep.

Ram, on the branch, did not sleep. He looked down and said, 'I wish I was back in the meadow with my flock.'

Donkey said, 'I'm getting cramp. I must move my legs. If I don't move my legs soon, I'll die.'

Renard was very cross. 'If you start moving about now, you'll risk falling off your perch. Then where will you be?'

'But my legs are in agony,' said Donkey, 'I must move.'

'Me too,' said Ram. 'My legs are in agony as well.'

'Go on then, do it,' snapped Renard. 'But it'll serve you right if you fall.'

Ram and Donkey fidgeted around on their branches trying to get comfy and, sure enough, both lost their balance and fell. But instead of crashing to the ground, they fell on top of the sleeping wolves. Donkey squashed four, and Ram killed another two. The rest of the pack were so terrified to see six of their team felled at a blow that they fled in panic. Renard, still in the tree, shouted at Ram to give chase. When the last wolf was out of earshot, he came down.

'There we are, good friends,' he said. 'I told you I'd take good care of you all the way. And here we are safe and sound, not a scratch on any of us.'

'I'm fed up,' said Ram. 'I'm not going any further on this pilgrimage. I'm going home.'

'Me too,' said Donkey.

The forest all around was dark and full of enemies. Renard said, 'You're probably right, friends. Any fool can walk to Rome and believe he's better for it. But east, west, home's always best. So best foot forwards for home.' And he ran and caught up with Ram and Donkey who'd already started the return journey.

Renard and the Eels

WHILE the cold weather lasted there was less to eat for all the animals. And that included Renard. There wasn't so much as a mouthful of anything anywhere. And to be starving was, in Renard's experience, a mortal inconvenience to say the least.

Renard slunk away from his lair, sunk deep in gloom, dumps, doldrums, and blues.

'Nothing to eat,' he moped to himself. 'Nothing to spend, nothing to comfort oneself with. Nothing to give to a friend in need — if one happened to feel in the mood for giving something to a friend.'

Renard's tail hung low. More than anything, he was miserably ashamed that he had nothing to feed to his wife and children.

He crept down to the river and checked out the reed beds but times were so hard that he didn't get so much as a sniff of a coot, let alone a duck or a goose. As the inconvenience of hunger began to grip his

stomach more tightly, he felt obliged to go and hang around by the road which the people used, in the hope that better luck would come his way.

And, in time, it did.

As he crouched behind a holly hedge, he saw a cart, laden with a fine catch of fish come bowling down the road. Renard saw and smelled a dozen baskets in the back of the cart, each filled to the brim with herrings, sprats, mackerels, lampreys, and eels. The one slight nuisance was that the two men who had made this magnificent haul were also on the cart, sitting up at the front. So, although the cart passed within a hair's breadth of Renard's nose, he couldn't do anything about the splendid eels except watch them trundle by.

However, as Renard knew, a bird in the hand is worth two in the bush, and the same goes for eels on a cart. So, keeping well hidden, he ran along the ditch beside the road till he'd overtaken the cart. Then, when he was well ahead, he quickly slipped out onto the road and lay down in the middle as though he was dead.

Renard was extremely good at this sort of thing. He closed his eyes, clenched his teeth as though *rigor mortis* had set in, and held his breath.

Along came the cart, and was forced to a stop just in front of Renard's lifeless body.

'Oi! I say, what's this 'ere thing, then? Lying there in the way?' said one of the men on the cart. 'Looks like some kind of monster. Wild boar, maybe? Or a mad dog? Better watch out.'

The other man said, 'It's a fox, you halfwit! Don't you know a fox when you see one. Dead by the look of it. Come on, quick, let's get it before anyone else sees it. That skin should be worth a tanner or two.'

Both men jumped down from the cart and ran towards Renard.

'Hey, watch it, you stupid idiot!' said one of the men to the other. 'It might not be quite dead yet. Might have the rabies. You don't want to get bitten.'

But Renard, stretched out on the road, his head thrown back, his breath held in, had no intention of biting anyone. And the two men, seeing him so dead, weren't afraid after all. They knelt down and inspected the brown fur on his back, and the white fur on his throat and breast.

'Worth more than a tanner or two, I'd say. Couple of quid if we're lucky. Bit of nifty bargaining.'

'God's truth, man! Only a couple of quid. More like a fiver, I'd say. Look at that underbelly! Really clean and white. Not a mark on him. Chuck him in the back.'

They picked up Renard and threw him in the back of their cart on top of the fish baskets.

'We can't do nothing about it now but we'll skin him this evening,' said one of the men.

'Yeah,' said the other. They were both pleased with themselves and with their good fortune.

Renard lying doggo on the baskets just behind them, said nothing but smiled to himself. 'Don't count your chicks before they're hatched, nor your foxes before they're skinned,' he thought.

Very quietly he ripped open the lid of one of the baskets with his sharp teeth and, as quick as lightning, he gobbled down one basket of herrings, that is to say, thirty of them, each one so succulent, so silvery,

47

so shiny and so sea-fresh, that Renard didn't mind in the least that he had no salt or vinegar or sage sauce to go with them.

Having had such a good catch with the first basket, he decided to cast his net again and, easing his nose under the lid of a second basket, he pushed and wrestled with his muzzle against the wicker until he managed to break it open. This one was full of eels strung together on loops of twine like necklaces. He slipped his nose through one loop of eels, then with a backward flick of his head, jerked the whole string over his back so that it hung round his shoulders like a cape with the eels dangling all round like ermine tails.

Escaping with his eel-cape was a little tricky, especially as there was no step down from the back of the cart, but he took a flying leap over the tailboard and landed safely.

'May God keep you, kind sirs,' he called to the two men as he scampered for cover. 'And thank you for my fine catch. I've only taken one stringful and as a token of my esteem, I've left all the rest for you. Oh, and thanks for the ride too.'

The men, hearing his call, immediately stopped the cart, and turned round.

'Good God! It's that ruddy fox. And he's jumped out!' said one man.

'Oi, you! Fox! Stop!' said the other.

'Damned deceiving swine,' muttered the first. 'We should've realized at the start he was only out to trick us. They always do, those foxes. It's in their nature.'

When they saw that not only had Renard escaped, but that he'd stolen some of their eels, they were furious and jumped down from their cart and began to run after him. But Renard hoped never to suffer the shame of being caught by men and so, even though hampered by the dangling eels, he didn't slow down for a second, and in the end the furious men had to let him go.

'Hope to God he dies of indigestion on that lot!' said one.

'Yeah, serve him right,' said the other, 'if his guts twist up.'

'Dear sir, please don't be angry,' Renard called over his shoulder. 'I'm not out to pick a quarrel. I'm just a dear friendly old fox who always minds his own business if he can.'

This last remark only made the two men angrier than ever and both took it out on the other. As he pranced away through the trees, Renard could hear them still arguing, each blaming the other for losing the fox and the eels.

When Renard reached his lair, his wife and cubs were extremely pleased to see him back with a good supper for them. His wife skinned and sliced the eels and Renard blew up the fire ready for the cooking. Then, just in case the sweet smell of sizzling fish should lure Wolf or Bear or Cat or Dog or any other greedy whingeing creature round in the hope of a mouthful, Renard wisely barred the entrance to the lair so that he and his family could enjoy their supper without the annoyance of neighbours.

Renard and the Rooster

O N a fine spring morning Renard went to a farmhouse he knew of which was on the far side of a wood. At this farm there were lots of hens and cockerels, donkeys, geese, ganders, goslings, and bantams. The admirable farmer who lived there also kept capons, ducklings, drakes, and pullets. Indoors, he had salt meat, sides of bacon, hams, and preserves. In his barn, he had good stores of corn. He had cherry trees and a well-kept apple orchard.

Renard liked going there to cheer himself up if ever he felt a bit peckish, which was of course possible not only in spring, but at any season. However, the yard where all the excellent hens, cocks, ducks, and geese lived was more like a fortified keep, for it was enclosed by a high oak fence and, as if that wasn't enough, it was also surrounded by a hedge of hawthorn making it doubly secure.

Renard, keeping a low profile, walked round the tough outer hawthorn hedge, but he could see no way of getting under, or over, or through the thick, tough, prickly, double barricade. Even if he took a mighty running jump over the top, he calculated that he'd come down on the other side from such a great height that the poultry would easily catch sight of him in his descent and rush for cover.

He crouched in the track just outside the inpenetrable yard, feeling angrier and angrier at himself. He had to find a way in. He had to have a hen, one of those dear contented hens which he could see and hear through the lattice of hawthorn prickles, yet could not reach.

Without making a sound, Renard prowled right round the outer perimeter. Then he went round it again, keeping low and quiet. And again, six times in all. And then, on the seventh time round, he gave a cry of triumph as he discovered a place where the fence was weak. One of the oak palings was slightly broken, making a small opening through which he was able to squeeze. And, just inside this part of the yard, was a nicely tilled cabbage patch full of firm bushy cabbages. Quickly, Renard flattened himself to the ground, hiding under the large leaves of the cabbages, though not before some of the hens had noticed his arrival. They became excited and anxious.

Their cock had been enjoying a pleasant dust bath on the far side of the farmyard but hearing his troupe making so much fuss, he strutted over to find out what was upsetting them, and why they'd all scurried over to cower against the farmhouse wall.

Pauline, most world-wise of the hens, who laid the largest eggs, and who was Number One wife, said, 'We were frightened, darling.'

'But why, my dearest one? What did you see to frighten you?'

'Some kind of wild beast. We thought it might hurt us.'

'Calm down, my dearest. It's just your imagination,' said Cock kindly. 'So long as I'm here to take care of you, you're all right.'

'But I *saw* something! We all did! You *must* believe me,' Pauline said.

51

'Very well then. You just tell me, quite calmly, in your own words, exactly what it was you think you saw.'

'We saw the cabbage leaves shaking and shivering.'

'Pauline, you're just letting your imagination run away with you. Now calm down. Stop panicking. You're only upsetting the others. You just go back and get on with your own business.'

And Cock went back to his own business which was to enjoy his dust bath, unperturbed by Pauline's silly panic. Little did he suspect what lay in store for him that fine spring day.

His *toilette* complete, he flew up onto the barn roof, took up a good position overlooking his troupe and, with one eye closed, but the other open, stood guard. But he soon grew bored of just standing there, so he tucked one leg comfortably under him, and in the warm spring sunshine, he had a bit of shut-eye.

And while he was snoozing, he began to dream. And this is what he dreamed.

Cock's Dream

Cock stood on the roof of the barn in the warm spring sun. He realized that, from the corner of the courtyard, Something was advancing towards him. He could not tell what this Something was. He knew only that it held out for him a red fur cloak which was fringed all round with two rows of little white bones. The underside of this strange garment was white.

The Something made Cock put on this curious outfit, helping him into it where it was too tight, Cock wondered why he had to put the garment on, and he felt uncomfortable because he seemed to have got the garment on back-to-front and upside-down so that it was chafing and constricting his body. He struggled about to make it less tight, but the more he struggled, the more constricting it seemed to become and he felt that he was beginning to suffocate.

Wearing the dream garment was so hot and disagreeable, that Cock woke up.

He was so relieved to find himself awake and to find that it was all only a dream that he said a quick thanksgiving prayer.

'Dear God, Holy Ghost, Saint Francis, Saint Hubert, Saint Julian, and all the other saints, deliver me from evil, and keep my body always safe. Amen.'

Then, he flew down to his hens and called Pauline to one side.

'Pauline, my dear, I think you may have been right to be worried about being dragged off by some strange creature.'

'Oh, no!' cried Pauline. 'Dearest one, you shouldn't say such things. It's bad to get all worked up by one's imagination. You told me so yourself. It's like our farmer's dog who's always yelping with pain before its master's even thought of giving it a beating. Look what a beautiful day this is. Warm, and sunny, and safe. What on earth can there be to be afraid of?'

'Pauline, while I was up there on the barn roof, I had a dreadful dream. If I tell you what happened in the dream, could you explain what it means? I dreamed that I saw a savage Something coming at me with a red-coloured fur coat which it forced me to get into. The hem of the garment was made of lots of little white things like bones, and the neck of the garment was hard and narrow and awkward. And the whole outfit seemed too small for me. Oh, it was such a vivid dream, it seemed to be real.'

'My dear, I know exactly what the Official Dream Interpreter would have to say about it and, by Saint Francis, I can only hope that for all our sakes, it isn't true. The garment you saw with the red fur is the fox himself. He was forcing *you* inside his own pelt. The bone fringe you saw were his two rows of terrible white teeth that you'll have to pass as you go in. The tightness you felt was the beast's terrible mouth and throat through which you must pass. That dream was a prophecy of the future. I knew there was something evil in the air today, ever since I saw the cabbage leaves shaking. Your vision confirms my suspicions. Now listen, you'd better keep yourself somewhere safe for the rest of the day.'

'Oh, Pauline! What a daft old hen you are. Still on about the cabbages. I suppose you think it was the fox you saw there? Fancy you suggesting that I'd ever let myself be caught out by a fox! What an idea. Surely you know me better than that. I'm afraid, my dear, I can only take your version of my dream as a lot of old cock-eye.'

'Husband, I have only given you what you asked for. The official interpretation of your dream. Go and ask any fortune-teller and he'd give you the same account.'

But Cock had had enough of old wives' tales and he marched off to the dust-bath where the warm dusty comfort lulled away his troubles, and soon he was having another forty winks.

The moment Renard realized that Cock seemed to be dozing, he crept out from under the cabbages, slunk over to the dustbath, and pounced. But Cock had been only half asleep. He instantly recognized Renard as the awful Something from his dream. Quick as a wink, he squarked, shook his wings and flapped up to the top of the dung-heap.

Renard cursed himself for missing such an easy catch. Having failed by the Sudden Grab Method, he'd have to get him by some more subtle means. There was a bit of sharp practice involving flattery which he'd used once before, to trick another of the winged species. It had very nearly worked that time. This time, Renard resolved, he'd refine the technique to include a closed-eye trap.

'I'll have him by sundown if it's the last thing I do. Otherwise, all

that time I've just spent lying in the dirt under the cabbages will have been utterly wasted.'

Gently, he called to Cock. 'My dear Cock-a-doodle. Please don't be so alarmed by my sudden movement. I was just so happy to see a cousin, safe and well.'

Cock felt slightly reassured to hear that Renard's intentions were not necessarily bad, though it was the first he'd heard of any family relationship.

'Yes, we're distantly related cousins,' said Renard. 'And blood's always thicker than water.'

Cock trilled an ode to spring.

'You know, cousin Cock, I remember your dear old dad. One of the champion Cock-a-doodle-doers of all time. No rooster crowed as well as he did. You could hear him at least a mile away. He crowed magnificently. His tone was good. He had a good long breath, and he could even sing with both eyes closed, so they said. In fact, some said he sang rather better with his eyes closed.'

'Fox, you aren't trying to play some kind of swizzle on me, are you?'

'What an absurd idea! Of course not. As a blood relation, I'd rather lose a leg of my own than think of any of my feathered family suffering in any way. I can honestly tell you, with my whole heart, that all I want is to hear you sing. To know if you sing better than your father.'

'Well, shove off a bit. Give me air. Give me a bit of breathing space. You're too close. If you move off a bit I'll sing so that there's not a neighbour in earshot who'll miss my lovely voice.'

'Make it good and loud, Rooster. Then they'll soon find out if you're really old cousin Cock-a-Doodle-do's son.'

Cock gave a splendidly loud long crow with one eye closed, though the other beady eye he fixed unblinkingly on Renard.

'Hm,' said Renard, when Cock had come to an end of his vocal outcry. 'Is *that* all you can do! Cousin Cock-a-doodle-do used to sing quite differently. It was louder, more melodious. He had a superb musical expression. His voice was somehow more tremolo, more vibrato, if I remember rightly. A good long blast with both eyes tight shut in total concentration. A sublime ululation. People used to hear him over twenty farms away.'

Cock too had heard this kind of praise told of his father. Since his father had long since turned to coq-au-vin, it seemed only right that he should now surpass his father's capabilities. He closed both eyes, threw back his head, and began to yodel with all his might as though his life depended on it.

Renard didn't waste a second. He hopped over some purple sprouting broccoli, rushed at Cock, seized him by the throat and bounded for cover. He felt extremely pleased with his speedy action.

But Pauline had seen.

'Husband, I told you so! I told you so!' she clucked. 'Now look! Now look! What'll we do? I told you so!'

At that same moment, the farmer's wife came to her kitchen door to start getting the hens cooped up before dusk.

'Daisy! Evie! Janie! Bertie! Pauline! Kissypoo!' She called the hens' names. 'Beddy-byes time!' And when they didn't come scurrying to her feet she was most surprised and called out for the cock who was supposed to be taking care of them. Then she caught sight of Renard, dragging Cock in his mouth. She ran to rescue the cock but Renard ran faster, and when she saw that she was losing ground, she began to shout for help. Some of the farm workers who were playing *boules* heard her and ambled over to see if they could help.

But her husband was angry.

'You stupid old cow!' he yelled. 'If you actually saw the fox with the cock in his mouth why didn't you get after him?'

'He was too fast.'

'Well why didn't you *hit* him with something, then?'

'I hadn't got anything to hit him with.'

'Well why didn't you use this stick, then?'

'He went faster than greased lightning.'

'Well which way did he go?'

'*That way!*'

The farmer and his workers rushed in the direction she pointed, yelling and shouting after Renard.

'Oi, you! Stop where you are. Drop that bird! This instant!'

Renard heard them and seeing a rat-run beneath the main barn, he dived in. The farmworkers saw him go.

'Oi, he went down there! After him!'

'Better watch it, fellows. We're dealing with an ugly customer.'

'Call up the dogs! Bardol! Traveller! Jupiter! Spot!'

'Fetch the terrier too!'

'And the ferret!'

'And if they can't get the stinking low-down trickster, we'll smoke him out.'

Cock, hanging helplessly in Renard's mouth, was not yet dead, though he knew he might be at any moment. It was his turn to think up a trick as quickly as possible if he was to save his skin.

'Oh poor Renard, cousin,' he croaked as best he could when his throat was being gripped by two rows of white teeth. 'What rude things those uncouth peasants are saying. What wretched plans that farmer has for you. I fear you're a marked man, already as dead as makes no difference. But I think I know what you could do to save yourself. You could give them one of your witty jokes! That'd really annoy them. When they say, "There he is!" and they're about to grab you, you shout back something really rude. What about, "And the same to you with brass knobs on"? That'd really surprise them.'

No fox is so cunning that he doesn't, once in a while, make a mistake. Renard made one now in following Cock's advice.

The men, the dogs and the ferret crowded round one end of the rat-run. Renard left by the opposite end and made straight towards the hole in the fence.

'There he goes! The stinker!' the men shouted.

'And the same to you with brass knobs on!' Renard shouted back.

The instant that Cock felt Renard's mouth open and the teeth loosen their grip, he struggled free, flapped his wings furiously, and flew up to the safety of an apple tree.

'Hello, now, down there, Renard!' he crowed, cock-a-hoop at his own cunning. 'And how's tricks then?'

Renard was appalled at how easily he'd been out-tricked by a simple farmyard fowl. 'If only I'd kept my mouth shut,' he snarled, trembling with rage.

'My cousin Renard, since that's what you wanted to call yourself (though it was a very silly idea to pretend we're related), if I were you I'd clear off from here pretty quick. Otherwise, you'll really be in the soup.'

As Cock anticipated, the men had briefly been taken aback at being insulted in their own farmyard by a thieving fox but their moment's hesitation was over.

'They're after you again,' Cock called. 'Why not give them another of your funny jokes?'

But Renard had no time for jokes. There'd already been far too much talking for one day.

'Silence is golden,' he thought to himself as he scrambled through the hole in the fence. 'I shan't ever speak another unneccessary word in my life.'

Renard Goes to Paradise

RENARD had a taste for poultry which hadn't been satisfied for some time. Then, in the barn belonging to the monastery, he found a whole flock of unattended hens and, since there wasn't a monk in sight, he quickly ate two and carried off another, well-dead, in his mouth in case he needed a snack later on.

But good eating made him thirsty. So he hid his snack in a safe corner of the barn and ran over to help himself to a quick drink of water from the well which stood in the middle of the courtyard just opposite the barn doors.

When he climbed up onto the edge of this well, he saw that the water level was way below his reach. He also saw, in the circle of white water at the bottom, another strange fox staring up at him.

Renard, not knowing about reflections of oneself at the bottom of wells, mistook it for a rival who had somehow got to the water first. Renard barked down at this other fox and the other fox seemed to bark back. Renard didn't know that it was his echo barking at him.

He was curious about what this other fox was up to, lurking and

61

barking at the bottom of the monastery well, so in order to get a better look, he stepped carefully onto a bucket which was dangling on a pulley rope. The moment that he'd put the weight of his well-fed body onto the bucket, he felt himself being suddenly plunged downwards through darkness. As he went down, an empty bucket which had been at the bottom of the well, rattled up past him to the top.

Renard's bucket jerked to a stop. Renard held out his paws to steady himself against the sides of the well. It was dark, damp, cold, and very frightening to find oneself so suddenly at the bottom of a well with water slopping around on all sides. Not unlike being buried alive, Renard thought.

'What a silly clot I was to get into this bucket. I should've known what would happen.' He sat, wedged in the bucket, wondering how on earth he was going to get himself up to ground level again.

Now, Wolf had also been out hunting that day and he too came through the monk's courtyard. He had caught nothing. He felt bearish with hunger. He leaned weakly against the side of the well.

Then, just like Renard before him, he noticed a reflection at the bottom and, like Renard, instead of realizing it was himself, he believed it to be a rival. He was not pleased. After all, he was supposed to be pack leader round here, though from the way some of them treated him, it was hard to believe.

Also down there, obviously plotting something with the stranger, Wolf saw Renard. Wolf hated Renard's guts more than anything in the world, ever since the time Renard had jammed his head in his own front door.

'Not *you* again!' Wolf shouted down the well. 'What in hell's name are you doing? Lord, if I could get my hands on you I'd shake the living daylights out of you!'

Just as Renard's bark had echoed back up to him like the call of another fox, so did Wolf's growling abuse echo back to him.

'Not *you* again!' Wolf heard. 'What in hell's name are you doing? Lord, if I could get my hands on you I'd shake the living daylights out of you!' And Wolf was so angry that any creature should dare speak to him like that, that he went on roaring and shouting more insults down the well.

'Who are you with down there? What are you doing? You reprobates! You good-for-nothings! I can see you, so don't pretend you're invisible.'

Renard, all this time, kept quite still in his bucket and didn't say a word. At last, when Wolf had worn himself out with screaming insults and hearing them repeated back, Renard called up:

'Dear Wolf, don't get worked up. It's only your dear old enemy, Renard, down here. You remember, Renard the trickster, who used to get up to so many naughty practical jokes. But now it's a case of the late departed trickster Renard. You'll never believe this Wolf, old friend, but I'm dead now.'

'Hm,' said Wolf. 'Well that's some comfort to me anyhow. Save me the trouble of finishing you off myself, because I never did care for you. Not one bit. Tell me, er, late departed Renard, how did you come to pass on to the happy hunting ground of the hereafter? That is to say, the new Jerusalem, I mean, ah, hem, aha, er, how long have you been, er, well, dead?' This was not a word Wolf, or any other animal, liked having to use.

'Funny you should ask me,' Renard called up in reply. 'Not so

63

long, as it happens. It was a surprise to me too, to go so soon. But after all, one's destiny is all in God's hands. One departs when he pleases. All part of the Great Plan. His privilege to give life and to take away. Ours not to reason why. But please, Wolf, don't fret about me. Dear kind God's taking excellent care of me now. Good old God. By the way, Wolf, I do hope that now I've gone over to the other side, to a far far better place, you'll try and forgive me from the bottom of your heart for all the rotten things I may have done to you. Specially about that unfortunate event the other day when you managed to get your head stuck in a door. It's been on my mind to ask you how you are. Though I dare say you've forgotten all about it by now. Ever so sorry, chum.'

'Well, that's all right, I suppose, now that you're dead and gone,' said Wolf. 'I'll forgive you if I must.'

'Oh what joy! Joy, joy, joy! Ever increasing happiness be always ours,' crooned Renard.

'Joy? What d'you mean? How can you be joyful? I thought that you were dead? Isn't that just about the worst thing of all that can happen to any of us?'

'Not at all, old friend. My body may be decaying in a coffin in some hole in the ground. But my spirit is right here in heaven. I've found everlasting bliss at the bottom of this well. I feel almost sorry for you creatures still stuck up there on earth, while here I am down in the heavenly well. In Elysian fields which are full of nice plump hens and docile ducks just waiting around quite patiently for me to get my teeth into them. I've never had it so good. And as for creatures of your inclination, there's sheep and goats just standing around. It really is pretty fantastic down here.'

'Well I never!' Wolf shouted down the well. 'I never knew heaven was like that. And I never knew it was down either. I always thought it was up.'

'Doesn't that just show you how wrong you are! Ah, Wolf, if only you could see the meadows as I see them, full of tender young lambikins, skipping merrily about and not a shepherd or a sheepdog in sight.'

'Don't tell me about it,' Wolf groaned. 'I'm so hungry I can't bear to hear any more. Oh, how I wish I could be right down there beside you this very minute.'

'Really?' said Renard. 'You do surprise me. Beside me down here? In spite of all the practical jokes I've played on you? What a good soul you are, to be so truly forgiving to a fellow creature. Unfortunately, Wolf, even if you wanted to be down here, they wouldn't let you in. You see, the Elysian fields of the hereafter aren't for anybody. To be allowed into heaven you have to have been really wicked, and then suddenly decide you're sorry about it. You've doubtless been *wicked* enough in your time, like when you were trying to get the better of me. Don't think I didn't know. But are you prepared to be *sorry* enough, I wonder?'

'Yes, yes, yes!' cried Wolf, drooling at the thought of those plump lambs jumping in Elysian fields. 'You're right. I *have* thought cruel thoughts about you. But now I'm terribly terribly sorry.'

'Well,' said Renard doubtfully. 'The problem is, there's only one way to get to paradise and that's by bucket.'

'By bucket!' Dimly, Wolf recalled some other event to do with a bucket which had not ended well, but his memory was poor and he couldn't remember the details.

'Now, see the bucket there, swinging on the rope? The empty bucket? Well it's a clever new invention of God's. You can only fit in the bucket when you've got rid of every single naughty thought, because you see, there wouldn't be room in that bucket for both you and your sins. Ah, Wolf, if only you could see all that tender juicy food just waiting. But are you really ready to confess everything?'

'Yes.'

'Like that time you said that your one and only aim in life was to throttle me if you could?'

'Yes. Do hurry up and let's get on with it.'

'And like that other time round at your place, when me and Donkey and Ram were enjoying a perfectly reasonable evening's singing, and you said you wouldn't let us leave your house alive, not after we'd eaten all your meat and drunk all your beer?'

'Yes,' said Wolf impatiently. 'I confess.'

'And do you also confess what you said about five minutes ago about how you'd do anything to get hold of Renard and shake the living daylights out of him?

'I've already said I confess everything I've ever done. Now just tell me what to do next.'

'You must say your prayers in true humility and simplicity. Are you kneeling down, reverently, and saying them?'

'Yes, I will. I mean, I am.' Wolf couldn't remember if you were meant to kneel with your hind legs or your front, so he went down on all fours. 'Our Father, shiny halo. Hubbledum de day name,' he mumbled, for this was the only bit he could remember of the Lord's Prayer. 'Amen. Yes, done my prayers now.'

'Good, then I expect you can already begin to see the beauty of the flickering candles, and hear the timeless harping of the angels, and the sweet voices of the massed choir? Oh, Wolf, it really is so tremendous, isn't it? Now listen carefully for the last bit. All you have to do now is just hop into the bucket up there and you'll be down in a trifle.'

Wolf struggled to fit his great bulk into the small bucket, first his two feet, then his bottom, then all of him and, since he was much heavier than Renard, his bucket immediately started to descend the well while Renard, in the other bucket, began to come up. And for a moment they were level as their buckets passed each other. Wolf called out, 'Renard! Why are you coming up?'

'Don't worry about a thing. I'll explain it all later. It's all quite natural, part of the system. When one soul goes down, another must come up. Just a curious custom of the place. I go up to paradise on earth while you go down to the devil in hell and I'm afraid you'll find it's not much cop down there. Damn glad I am to get out of that hole!'

As soon as it reached the top of the well, Renard leaped out of his bucket, ran to find his spare hen hidden in the barn, and then trotted off home, leaving Wolf to his fate at the bottom of the deep dark well.

And he didn't have to stay there much longer. One of the monks came out to fetch water for the monastery and couldn't understand why the bucket was too heavy to pull up. So we went and fetched the monastery donkey and three more monks to help. They made the donkey pull on the rope. But however much they threatened him and whacked him and however hard the donkey strained, he still couldn't

pull up the bucket. One of the monks looked down into the well to see what the matter was. He saw Wolf.

'Gracious me! There's a wolf in our well!' he said. 'I'll bet it's the one who's been killing all our sheep.'

He ran back to the monastery to fetch the rest of his holy brothers. The abbott told everybody to arm himself with a weapon. Some got hoes, some rakes, and the abbot had a club and the precentor picked up a candelabra and they all rushed out to the well-head with their weapons. They helped the donkey pull on the rope till the bucket reached the top.

Wolf scrambled out and tried to escape between their legs, but the monks beat him about the head and the monastery watchdogs snapped and snarled, until Wolf was so badly wounded that he fainted clean away and saw stars sparkling like the lights of heaven, and heard strange distant noises ringing in his ears like the singing of angels.

'He's good and done for,' said the abbott as Wolf sank unconscious to the ground.

The precentor took out his sheath knife and was about to remove Wolf's skin to make a nice fur rug for his cell to keep out the draughts in winter. But the abbott stopped him.

'Look, that pelt's not worth the effort. It's all torn and messed up,' he said, for it seemed to him that if anybody was going to get a nice wolfskin rug it should be him. 'Just dispose of the body over there in that thicket.' So the monks dragged Wolf's body away and flung it into a large bramble bush. Then they all went in to Evensong.

Wolf had just come to in the bramble bush and was beginning to lick his wounds when his son trotted by.

'Why, poor old daddy, what's happened to you?'

'My son, my son,' groaned Wolf. 'Renard betrayed me. He lured me down a well and told the monks to beat me up when I got out.'

Just thinking about it made Wolf's head swim again. He seemed to see stars and hear strange noises, and his son had to help him home.

Renard meanwhile was safely back in the lair with his family eating chicken supper, which was the closest thing to being in seventh heaven.

'I'm the brightest of them all,' thought Renard. 'There's not a creature on earth that's as smart as me.' Or so he thought.

Renard and the Fatty Sausage

RENARD and Cat were stalking along the same road, at the same time, and on the same day. There was no way that a meeting could be avoided.

'Why, hello, there,' called out Renard, who disliked Cat almost more than any other creature he knew. 'Haven't seen you in these parts for a while. Great to see old pal Puss again. Long time no see, eh?'

'Er, what's that?' said Cat, surprised, because the last time they'd met, there had been claws drawn and fur flying.

'Always good to meet a friend,' said Renard. 'A gentleman and a friend one might almost say. A friend *in need* is a friend *indeed*.'

He fell into step with Cat.

'Can't trust a soul these days, can one?' said Renard, trotting down the track by Cat's side. 'Rogues and scoundrels everywhere. You know, Cat, I've a good mind to let the past be the past because you and I ought to stick together. As comrades in arms. What about a gentleman's agreement, just the two of us? I promise, Scout's honour, cross my heart and hope to die, that from now on, I'll be your faithful colleague.'

'Very well,' said Cat.

'Go on then, you have to say it too. After me: eternal friend Renard, you say, I promise that through thick and thin, in sickness and in health, for richer, for poorer, through good times and lean, till death do us part, we're best pals. Amen.'

Cat repeated it, though he suspected that Renard had no intention of keeping his side of such a ridiculous promise.

They trotted on down the path, side by side.

Soon, both began to feel hungry and, like all meat-eating predators, both began to keep an eye open for a likely meal. And suddenly, both caught sight of an enormous pork sausage lying beside the path as though a miracle had placed it there for them to find. Both leaped for it. Renard got there first.

'Hey, you fox!' snarled Cat. 'I hope you're going to share that!'

'Why of course I am,' said Renard politely. 'We're best friends.

'Get on with it then. I'm hungry.'

'Keep calm,' said Renard. 'If we eat it here, in the open, some other greedy pig is sure to come along and want a bit. We ought to take it somewhere quieter.'

He held the sausage firmly between his sharp teeth and, with the ends flopping down on either side of his muzzle, began to run rapidly ahead. Cat kept close behind.

'It's disgusting to see what you're doing to our sausage,' said Cat. 'The middle bit's covered in dribble from your mouth and the ends are trailing in the dust. If you go on carrying it like that, I'll refuse to eat with you. You ought to carry it the proper way.'

'And what *is* the proper way to carry a sausage?' Renard mumbled, between closed teeth because he had no intention of letting go the prize.

'Give it here and I'll show you,' said Cat.

Renard didn't really want to let Cat anywhere near the sausage. On the other hand, it occurred to him that if Cat were to carry it, he'd be so weighed down that it would be easy to knock him for six. Then, while

Cat sprawled on his back, he could grab the sausage back and make off with it. For this reason and this reason only, Renard allowed Cat to take hold of it.

'It's only fair,' said Cat, 'that we should take turns to carry our precious burden.' And most skilfully, as though he'd been transporting enormous sausages all his life, Cat gripped one end between his teeth and swung the rest over his shoulder and balanced it along his back.

'See, Renard, this way it can't drag in the dirt and get all mucky. Nor am I slobbering all over it like you were. A little *savoir-faire* helps in these matters, you know.'

Ahead of them Cat noticed a large wooden cross on top of a grassy mound. 'We'll make for that little hill, and eat it there, where we can see all round and make sure no one else is coming. Okay?'

'Very well,' said Renard, for he saw nothing suspicious about this plan.

But immediately, Cat put on tremendous speed, shot off along the track and didn't stop till he'd reached the grassy mound where, being a cat and good at climbing vertical posts, he scrambled up the wooden cross and settled down on one of the arms.

Renard was extremely annoyed at being out-tricked so easily, especially by a mere mog.

'Hey, you! You stinking tomcat! What are you up to! Come back here!' he barked as he galloped after him.

'No tricks, my dearest,' purred Cat sweetly. 'I just wanted to make sure that our sausage was out of harm's way. Now come on up and let's get feasting.'

Angrily, Renard sat down at the foot of the cross. He knew that Cat knew that foxes can't climb posts, or fences or stockades because their claws can't grip into wood like a cat's claws can.

'You must come on down,' he howled. 'This instant! Otherwise, it's not fair. You know I can't come up. And if you don't come down you might at least throw me down my share. After all, it was me that found it. Then we'll be all fair and square and you needn't ever be nice to me again.'

'What d'you take me for? D'you think I'm nutty, or drunk, or something? I wouldn't come down for a thousand pounds,' said Cat

and, holding the sausage firmly with his paws, he began to devour the rich fatty meat. 'Besides, my devoted friend,' he went on, 'you know as well as I do the value of our sacred sausage. It's holy meat. And you know how it can only be eaten in a holy place, either in church, or sitting on a cross. Otherwise, it's blasphemous. Honour the holy sausage! On your knees.' He gobbled down a bit more. 'Ah, most holy relic,' he muttered. 'Exalted, precious, hallowed meat. I name thee Sausage.'

'Oh, sausage,' Renard wailed from below.

'That's right,' murmured Cat. 'Blessed be its holy name. Honi soit qui mal y pense. That's Latin, you know. Sausage, sausage. Saying the word is like a prayer. Sausage, sausage. In the name of the sausage, the sausage, and holy sausage, Amen.'

'Just throw me down a morsel. I beg you.'

'How can you *possibly* ask, Renard, to dishonour the holy sausage by throwing it down to the ground! You're so disrespectful of everything that we ought to hold sacred! But I'll tell you what we *could* do, as one believer to another. The very *next* sacred sausage we find shall be all yours, to yourself. No question of having to share with anybody else! How's that for a bargain?

Renard could hardly bear to hear the sound of Cat's jaws tearing at the sausage skin, chewing the crumbs of pig. 'Pussy, oh dear Pussy, dearest Mog of all! Just a tiny taste, please pass me down the smallest speck.' Renard was so desperate that he began to weep real tears of self-pity, and Cat, having practically finished, peered down at his life-long persecutor.

'Aha! I'm glad to see that you cry tears of remorse for your many sins,' he purred with delight. 'I'm sure our dear Lord will notice how you repent and forgive you.'

Renard saw how Cat had very nearly finished the entire treasure, and groaned with despair. But then a more hopeful thought occurred to him. 'You up there, polecat!' he called. 'You'll have to come down soon because you're going to be really thirsty after all that guzzling.'

'Oh, no, I won't,' said Cat airily. 'You see, God cares for me in a very special way, providing for all my needs. He's very conveniently left me useful little puddles of rainwater in the cracks in the wood. Just enough to quench a cat's thirst. So it'll probably be ages before I decide to come down.'

'In that case, I declare that our oath of friendship is null and void. In its place I'm making a new promise, in deadly earnest this time. I swear, on my grandmother's grave and on everything else I hold holy, that I'm not budging from here till you come down. And then, by golly, I'll get you. Ha! Ha! So you see, you're well and truly trapped.'

'Nicely spoken, Renard', said Cat, licking his lips and then his paws. 'There's only one little problem. You haven't eaten for some while and I happen to know you're feeling pretty hungry. So just suppose I decide to stay up here for some time? Say seven hours? Or seven days? Or seven weeks? You're not going to manage to fast all that time. Still, that's your look-out, not mine. So I'll just sit here and meditate,' and he settled himself comfortably down and began to purr loudly.

Renard trembled and twitched with fury at Cat's wretched cunning.

But then, above the purring, he heard another noise which made his heart freeze with terror. He heard the far-off baying of dogs on the rampage.

Cat heard it too. 'Do you hear what I hear?' Cat said softly. 'Sweet and distant music of happy hounds? A congregation of pilgrims processing across the countryside, tearing through thickets, sniffing under hedges, racing across fields, chanting their masses and matins. And when they reach my special cross they'll sing a beautiful requiem for the dead. I'll bet you'll want to stay around for that, being such a holy fox.'

Renard knew he was in a tight spot. Any moment now the hounds would pick up his scent. If he kept his oath and waited for Cat to come down, he'd be skinned alive the moment they were onto him.

'Why, Renard,' said Cat, 'do I see you making preparation for a speedy retreat from this holy place?'

'Urgent business. All of a sudden,' said Renard.

'Got to go? For the sake of Gabriel and all the other angels, don't break your vow. You swore to sit tight till I come down. You can't go breaking promises like that or else I'll sue you for breach of contract. I'll call you trickster, petty criminal, cheat, swindler, and perjurer. But tell you what, I'm on good terms with the dogs. I could arrange a truce with them, so they won't hurt you, I could get you a guarantee of safe conduct. Now how about that, as one pal to another?'

But Renard knew he couldn't trust Cat's guarantee of a truce with the dogs any more than he'd trust his own promises and oaths. So he cantered away to take cover in the safety of the woods.

Once his escape from the hounds was sure, he made one more solemn promise, to himself this time. He vowed that if ever he met that cat again, there'd be no peace talks, no truces, no friendship, only direct confrontation and open combat.

Renard and the Blue-tit

NOBODY but the meanest, leanest dog ever wanted to eat Renard. His flesh was too sour. But Renard, on the other hand, always wanted to eat everybody else.

Today, though starving, and aching all over with hunger, he walked along the path trying to look his sleek and handsome best. For he was going to play a new special trick he'd never tried before, and he was going to try it on the smallest and prettiest of all the birds, the blue-tit.

There she was, sitting on the old oak tree, trilling to the sun.

'Morning, darling!' Renard called up. 'Lovely to see you enjoying the summer. Won't you come down and give me a kiss, my sweetheart?'

'Now then, don't you be saucy. We'll have none of that hanky-panky!' replied Blue-Tit.

'Not a saucy kiss, just a little kiss for old times' sake.'

'Old times' sake? And what times is that? You've done more damage to more birds than I've laid eggs. In fact it's high time you began to pull yourself together, young man. Otherwise, I simply don't know what's to become of you.'

'Dear and charming Mrs Blue-tit, if not for old times' sake, then how about a kiss for the sake of my godson, your son, Master Blue-tit? After all, I was present at his baptism.'

'And a fat lot of good you've been as a godfather, promising to take care of his moral welfare.'

'Dearest madam, if you won't kiss for old times' sake, nor for the sake of my godson, then at least a kiss for the sake of simple friendship that exists between one member of the animal kingdom and another.'

'What friendship is that?'

'The friendship between all creatures that on earth do dwell. Didn't you know that our noble king has just ordered everlasting peace among all creatures?'

'Everlasting peace? It's the first I've heard of it.'

'Between all the animals, great and small. And all your lot are terribly pleased about it.'

'What d'you mean, "Our lot"?'

'All you little people. Birds and bats, voles and field mice. Because you see, it now means that we bigger ones aren't going to pick quarrels with your lot ever again. All of us will live together in perfect harmony, just as we did at the beginning of the world when we first came out of the sea. So please, my dear sweet and lovely Mrs Blue-tit, it is up to each one of us to practice what the king has ordered. So let us share a kiss of peace, a little peck on the cheek. Nothing saucy. The past is the past. Long live the King.'

'Well, I'm afraid there's going to be none of that round here, my lad.'

Renard ached with hunger. And Blue-tit was harder to convince than he had expected.

'Listen, my dear. Obviously, with my past reputation, you're quite right to be a bit suspicious. So I know what. I'll close my eyes and then you can kiss me.'

He closed his eyes and waited.

So Blue-tit picked up a wisp of soft moss in her beak and swooped down towards the fox. But instead of kissing him, she gently stroked the moss against his whiskers. As soon as he felt the soft touch near his jaw,

he made a quick snip-snap. But all he managed to catch between his teeth was a dry mouthful of moss.

He opened his eyes in time to see Blue-tit safely back up on her branch. She was ruffled and angry.

'You cheat!' she cheeped. 'What kind of peace is it when you snap at me like that. You practically bit my tail off. I thought you said it was peace everywhere?'

Renard giggled. 'I was only having a bit of silly fun, Mrs Blue-tit. I wanted to kiss you back. You know, kiss the girls and make them cry. I didn't mean it seriously. Come on, let's do it again, only this time, let's both kiss properly. No cheating, either side. The past is the past and long live the King.' And he closed his eyes.

'Oh, very well then,' said Blue-tit and this time she came dangerously close to his muzzle, brushing right against him with her wing-tip. Renard, quick as lightning, snapped. Again, he was not as fast as she was.

Blue-tit jumped back to her branch, not only annoyed, but quite frightened.

Renard was furious with himself for being so slow.

'Darling, darling, Blue-tit, please don't be afraid,' he said gently. 'That was my silly old trick, to test your respect for me. And you have indeed won my respect. I promise, promise, promise, no more tricks. Just a kiss of friendship.'

Third time lucky, he thought.

But Blue-tit sat firm on the branch cheeping at the sun, ignoring Renard, refusing to listen to any more of his sweet-talk.

Renard ached with hunger and longing and tried to work out a new and final scheme. But then, in the distance, he heard that terrible sound of barking dogs. They were onto his scent after all.

Blue-tit glanced down from the oak tree and trilled at him.

'Peace among the animals, I thought you said. But I'm afraid those foxhounds don't sound too peaceful. Sounds more as though they've got it in for you, Renard. Hot on your trail, I'd say. And intending to break any peace just about as quickly as you broke it.'

The hunt was drawing nearer. Not only could they hear the yapping of the dogs, but the blowing of horns, and the thundering of horses' hooves.

'Darling, of course there's universal peace. It's just that those stupid young hounds don't yet know about the new law. They're only puppies.'

But as Renard knew, even puppies enjoy a good fight. He turned and dived into the undergrowth.

'Hey, come back, Renard!' Blue-tit trilled. 'What about the kiss of friendship? Really, what a way to treat a lady!'

But Renard wasn't there to hear. He'd disappeared without a trace. Hungry or not, he needed every bit of foxy cunning to save his skin.

But Renard the Fox always has another trick up his sleeve. He did get away safely and he did find something to eat. So, although this is the end of the book, it's not the end of Renard.

Goodnight. Sleep tight.
Mind the foxes don't bite.
But if they do, take a shoe
And beat them till they're black and blue.

Afterword

STORIES about the fox, the wolf, the crow, and the other animals have been collected and retold for centuries. Good stories change each time they pass from one story-teller to another. This is why different versions of the same story may be found in different parts of the world.

The twelve stories in this book have been chosen, adapted, and translated from *Le Roman de Renart*, a rambling collection of stories satirizing life and customs in medieval France, written in rhyming verse by a number of different poets, priests, and clerks between the years 1150 and 1250. This was a period of excitement and adventure in Europe, with an expansion in learning, literature and the arts. The Renard stories show a vigorous tradition of popular humour commenting on behaviour of kings, scholars, and churchmen. In the behaviour of the animals, we recognize many human characteristics and failings.

The Renard stories remained popular for many centuries because they combined realistic observation of the animal world with witty portrayal of human characteristics. Foxes are creatures of great cunning. For example, country people have observed foxes pretending to be dead or injured in order to catch a bird or a rabbit. The fox's cunning can seem very close to human hypocrisy, so when a medieval artist wanted to depict hypocrisy or treachery he would often show the fox tricking one of the other animals. Many examples of this survive from medieval times, especially on the carved pews and columns of ecclesiastical buildings. In the cathedrals of Bristol, Carlisle, Hereford, Ripon, and Peterborough, as well as in simple parish churches, carvings of Renard can be found. Keep a sharp look-out the next time you visit an old church. You may find Renard's beady eye fixed on you.